Please, Don't Eat My Cabin

Jean Merrill

Illustrated by Frances Gruse Scott

ALBERT WHITMAN & Company, Chicago

ISBN 0-8075-6551-2. LIBRARY OF CONGRESS CATALOG CARD 70-165818.
TEXT © 1971 BY JEAN MERRILL. ILLUSTRATIONS © 1971 BY FRANCES GRUSE SCOTT.
PUBLISHED SIMULTANEOUSLY IN CANADA BY GEORGE J. MCLEOD, LIMITED, TORONTO.
LITHOGRAPHED IN THE UNITED STATES OF AMERICA. ALL RIGHTS RESERVED.

*For Tessie and W. A. Gruse with fond memories
of happy summers at Clarion: the cool woods,
Tessie's hot cakes—and many porcupines!*

ADAM was a very friendly boy. Adam made friends with animals as easily as with people. And he was always bringing home a new animal for a pet.

So far, Adam had brought home twelve cats, a baby skunk, a rabbit, a turtle, a star-nosed mole, and a nice old goat that someone wanted to get rid of. All of Adam's animals were gentle and well-behaved. So Adam's mother couldn't fuss too much, even though the house sometimes seemed a little crowded.

In a way Adam's mother was proud of him. For not everyone can tame a star-nosed mole so that it will sit on one's shoulder and sleep in a sock pinned under one's bed.

The person who took the greatest interest in Adam's animals was his grandmother, Tessie. Whenever Tessie came to visit, she drew pictures of all of Adam's animals.

Tessie had a camp in the woods. One summer she invited Adam to visit her. He could bring his mole, she said.

In the woods where Tessie had her camp, there were deer and foxes and raccoons and opossums and many other animals that Adam had never seen. Adam planned to tame them all.

"Don't tame *too* many," said Adam's mother, as she put him on the bus with his suitcase and his star-nosed mole. "A deer would be too big to have around the house. Try not to tame anything bigger than a small raccoon."

"Don't worry," Adam said. "Anything I tame this summer, I'll give to Tessie. There's lots of room for animals at a camp."

Adam loved Tessie's camp. There were three
cabins in a clearing in the woods. Tessie slept
in one. Adam slept in another.

In the third and biggest cabin, Tessie and Adam
fixed their meals. The big cabin had a stone fireplace, and there were shelves around the sides,
where Tessie kept nice things that she had found
in the woods.

Down the hill from the big cabin was a spring-house, a little building over an ice-cold spring. Tessie used the springhouse to keep food cool and fresh in hot weather.

Tessie's camp was the kind of place where everyone did exactly what he felt like doing. Tessie collected flowers and ferns and mushrooms and painted pictures of them. And Adam explored the woods, looking for animals to tame for Tessie.

If Adam didn't feel like having breakfast—or coming back to camp for lunch—it was all right with Tessie. When Tessie was painting, she, too, often forgot it was time to eat. She and Adam ate when they felt like it.

Sometimes they didn't have dinner until nine o'clock at night. And if what they felt like having for dinner was popcorn and a pitcher of home-made grape juice, that's what they had.

In fact, they often had popcorn and grape juice, as it was their favorite dinner. Adam popped the corn in Tessie's fireplace, while Tessie recited funny poems that she had learned when she was a little girl in school.

THE FIRST MONTH that Adam stayed with Tessie, he tamed a field mouse and baby owl and a woodchuck for her.

Adam found the woodchuck in a trap a hunter had set. The woodchuck's leg was broken, and Adam put a splint on it. By the time the leg was mended, the woodchuck was very tame.

"I never knew of anyone taming a woodchuck before," Tessie said.

"You just have to be friendly," Adam said. "Animals can tell who their friends are."

Tessie liked the woodchuck best of all the creatures Adam had tamed. The woodchuck lay in the sun and kept her company while Adam was out in the woods looking for other animals to tame.

Tessie talked to the woodchuck a lot. She said that he understood everything she said.

ONE MORNING when Adam *did* feel like having breakfast, and he and Tessie were having a huge breakfast of whole-wheat hot cakes and honey and bacon and grape juice, Adam told Tessie about a strange gnawing sound that he had heard in the night.

"It couldn't have been the mouse," Adam said. "It was too loud a sound for the mouse. And it wasn't a woodchuck sound."

"No, it couldn't have been the woodchuck," Tessie said. "The woodchuck was sleeping in my cabin. I know because he kept my feet warm."

"And I'm pretty sure it wasn't the little owl," Adam said. "He sometimes scratches around on the beam in my cabin. Or he scruffles his feathers if something scares him. But this sound was more like a grinding, gnawing sound."

Tessie frowned. "Adam," she said, "I'm afraid it was a porcupine."

"A porcupine!" Adam said. He'd never seen a porcupine.

"I'll have to set a trap," Tessie said.

"You don't have to set a trap to catch him," Adam said. "I'll tame him for you."

"I don't want a tame porcupine," Tessie said. "I don't want a porcupine anywhere near my camp."

"A porcupine wouldn't hurt you, Tessie," Adam said. "Porcupines never attack people or other animals. They only use their quills if you attack them. So if I tame the porcupine, and he knows we're friendly. . . ."

"I don't plan to be friendly with a porcupine," Tessie said. "I'd like to trap every porcupine in this woods."

"Why?" Adam said.

"Because they've been trying to eat up my camp for years," Tessie said.

"How could they eat the camp?" Adam asked.

"They like to gnaw on wood," Tessie said. "Porcupines like a tasty piece of wood better than you like popcorn.

"Last summer," Tessie said, "porcupines gnawed

a hole in my cabin floor. And the year before, they
gnawed through three cornerposts of my springhouse, and the whole springhouse fell down. They
ate my outdoor benches, and they ate my favorite
outdoor drawing table that a friend made for me."

Tessie took Adam to the woodshed to show him
what was left of her favorite table.

"Porcupines," Tessie said, "have been known to gnaw holes in metal plates, plastic buckets, rubber hoses, saddles, shoes, automobile tires, battery cables, and road signs. They can even gnaw through glass bottles."

"Glass bottles!" Adam said. "They must have very sharp teeth."

"They do," Tessie said. "And if one of them is using his sharp teeth to gnaw a hole in your cabin, he better watch out."

Adam went to inspect his cabin. Sure enough. Something had been gnawing at the cabin door.

"You see," Tessie said. "So if I see a porcupine around here, I'm going to scream bloody murder. I'm going to whack him with a broom. And if I had a shotgun, I'd shoot him!"

"Would you really?" Adam said.

"Yes, I would," Tessie said.

"But maybe that's why a porcupine ate your table," Adam said. "Maybe the porcupines think you don't like them."

"I *don't*," Tessie said. "I like frogs and salamanders and beetles and birds. I like woodchucks and field mice. All the creatures in the woods are welcome in this camp—*except* porcupines."

Tessie looked sharply at Adam. "And don't you go taming one. A porcupine is no animal to be friendly with if you have a camp in the woods."

Adam was sorry to hear this. He was sure he could make friends with a porcupine. And if a porcupine was your friend, he wouldn't eat your cabin, would he? Or would he?

A FEW DAYS later, while Adam and Tessie were frying some parasol mushrooms that Tessie had found in a meadow near the camp, there was a shot in the woods. The woodchuck made a frightened sound and tried to climb into Tessie's lap.

Adam ran outside to see who was shooting.

A man walked out of the woods, carrying a dead
porcupine. The hunter was Tessie's friend Old Ben,
who had a camp a few miles up the road.

"Sorry to shoot so close to your camp, Tessie,"
Old Ben said. "But I know how you feel about
porcupines."

Adam kneeled down to look at the dead porcupine. He stroked its quills. To his surprise, they were soft to the touch, although they were needle-sharp at the tips.

"I bet I could have tamed him," Adam said to Old Ben.

"I bet that's the one that was gnawing on your cabin," Tessie said.

"Thank you," she said to Old Ben. "You can bury him in the vegetable garden."

Adam followed Old Ben out to the garden.

"I bet I could have tamed him," Adam said again, as he watched Old Ben dig a hole at the far end of the garden.

"Maybe you could have," Old Ben said. "People say porcupines do make nice pets. But I know how Tessie feels. She loves this camp. And she's always been afraid a porcupine might chew the whole thing down."

T HAT NIGHT Adam lay awake in his cabin for a
long time. He was wondering how he would
go about taming a porcupine if he ever got the

chance. He was just falling to sleep when he heard the whirr of wings over his head.

Something had startled the owl. It swooped twice around the cabin, then flew out the moonlit window.

Adam heard a whimpering sound. It sounded like a child crying. It was coming from inside the cabin. From somewhere over his head.

Adam felt for his flashlight and flashed it into the dark corners of the cabin. To his surprise, on a beam at one end of the cabin was a baby porcupine. It was about as big as a small cantaloupe.

The baby was moaning and whimpering as if its heart would break. Adam guessed that it was crying for its mother, the big porcupine that Old Ben had shot. The baby must have climbed in the cabin window.

Adam tiptoed out to the woodshed and got a ladder. He propped it against the beam of the cabin and climbed up to where he could reach the porcupine.

But he did not reach out for a minute. He just talked softly to the little animal in a comforting tone of voice.

"Don't be afraid, little guy," Adam said. "I won't hurt you. I'm your friend. Everything's going to be okay. Don't worry. Take it easy. Don't worry. Don't worry at all."

Adam kept talking in a low voice until the baby porcupine stopped crying. Then Adam sang a song that Tessie sometimes sang to herself as she was painting—

> *White sand and gray sand—*
> *Who'll buy my white sand?*
> *Who'll buy my gray sand?*

The porcupine made a long sighing sound. He looked as if he might just curl up and go to sleep there on the beam.

Adam wondered if the porcupine would raise his quills if he tried to pick him up. He reached out his hand very slowly. He was almost touching the porcupine's soft black nose.

Adam waited a second. The porcupine nosed forward and touched Adam's hand.

Adam stretched his hand further and gently stroked the bristly little back. The porcupine lay quietly on the beam.

Adam smiled to himself.

"Are you hungry?" he whispered.

Adam peeled a piece of loose bark from the cabin beam and held it out to the porcupine. The porcupine took the bark from Adam's hand and began to chew on it.

"Oh, oh," Adam said. "I thought maybe you'd be too little to eat a cabin."

Adam thought a minute.

"Wait," he said. "I'll get you something better to eat. But, please, don't eat the cabin while I'm gone."

Adam ran to the springhouse. He found an ear of sweet corn left over from supper and hurried back to the cabin.

The porcupine was asleep when Adam got back to the cabin.

"Good," Adam said. "You didn't eat the cabin."

Adam very carefully lifted the porcupine down from the beam and made a comfortable spot for him in the quilt on his bunk. He broke off a kernel of corn and offered it to the porcupine.

The porcupine sniffed at the corn. Then he took the kernel from Adam's fingers.

"See?" Adam said. "That's a lot better than cabins. Have another piece."

The porcupine ate another kernel. And then another. Then he reached out for the whole ear and held it in his forepaws and gnawed the corn from the cob, just as Adam would have done.

To Adam's astonishment, the porcupine ate the whole ear of corn. And when he had gnawed off the last kernel, he flopped over and fell asleep on Adam's bunk.

ADAM lay awake for a while, trying to think what to do about the baby porcupine. If someone had killed a baby's mother, it didn't seem right not to help the baby along until it was old enough to take care of itself.

It was clear to Adam that a porcupine could be tamed. But it was also clear that porcupines did like to eat cabins.

Maybe I could train him not to, Adam thought. I'm sure I could.

WHEN Adam woke up the next morning, the baby porcupine was still sleeping on the quilt beside him. The porcupine's belly was puffed out from his big midnight corn snack.

Adam tickled the little fellow's fat belly. The porcupine made a sleepy contented sound and snuggled closer to Adam.

Before he went to have breakfast with Tessie, Adam emptied out the suitcase he kept under his bunk. Then he put the porcupine in the suitcase.

"Until I'm sure you're trained," he said, "you better stay in here." The suitcase was made of a wicker material like a basket, so the porcupine could breathe.

"I'll bring you food to eat, and come and talk to you, and everything will be okay," Adam said. "And I'll bring some pine needles to make you a nice soft bed. Just trust me. And, please, don't eat the cabin."

By the end of two days, the little porcupine was as tame as the star-nosed mole. The mole wasn't sure he liked Adam's new roommate, and made a wide circle around the suitcase. But as the mole and the porcupine were both rodents, Adam was sure they would be good friends in time.

Adam decided to name the porcupine Q. Because every time he said "porcupine," the q-sound in the middle of the word came out the strongest.

Adam saved little bits of all the nicest things Tessie cooked and carried them to his cabin for Q. He also brought him fresh lettuce from the garden and mushrooms and the leaves of wild plants from the woods.

Q liked lima beans and popcorn and bits of bacon the best of all the things Adam fed him. When Adam gave him a piece of bacon, Q made a cooing sound.

"I'll bring you all the bacon you want," Adam said. "But, please, don't eat the cabin. *Promise that.*"

Sometimes Q seemed to answer Adam. He made more funny sounds than any pet Adam had ever had.

Besides the cooing sound, Q sometimes made a mumbling sound like an old man talking to himself. Sometimes he grunted. Sometimes he yipped. And sometimes when he was happy, it sounded as if he were singing. Some of the sounds Q made were so human that Adam often thought that there was another person in the cabin.

WHEN a couple of weeks had passed, Adam could see that Q was getting too big to stay in the suitcase. Every time Adam took him out to feed him, Q wanted to explore the cabin. And he kept trying to climb up to the open cabin window.

Adam decided that it was time to tell Tessie about the porcupine. Tessie was painting a picture of the woodchuck when Adam came up with Q following at his heels like a puppy.

"I have a surprise for you, Tessie," Adam said.

"What is it?" Tessie asked, looking up. Then she saw Q and screamed.

"Look out! There's a porcupine behind you."

"That's the surprise," Adam said. "His name is Q, and he's very tame. He's lived in my cabin for two weeks, and he hasn't eaten it. He'd rather eat bacon."

Adam picked up Q to show Tessie how tame and friendly he was.

"Be careful," Tessie gasped. "He'll stick you full of quills."

"No, he won't," Adam said. "He knows I'm his friend. See—he doesn't even bristle."

Adam explained to Tessie how he had found Q.

Tessie sighed. "Adam, what did I tell you about porcupines?"

"You told me you didn't want a tame porcupine," Adam said. "But he was crying for his mother when

I found him. And I thought maybe you'd change your mind if he didn't eat the camp. If there's enough bacon, I don't think he will."

Tessie put on her glasses and looked more closely at Q. Q rustled his quills slightly. Tessie stepped back nervously.

"He's not sure you like him," Adam said.

"Neither am *I*," Tessie said.

"Bacon is what he likes best," Adam explained. "But he likes lots of other things, too. Clover blossoms and mushrooms and carrots and milk and apples and popcorn and whole-wheat toast. But aren't you surprised that he likes bacon so much?"

"Bacon's salty," Tessie said. "That's why he likes it. Wild animals often can't find enough salt in the woods. That's why porcupines eat tables and chairs and cabins. Anything that's been touched by sweaty human hands has traces of salt on it."

Q reached out a paw and took hold of the paintbrush that Tessie had in her hand.

"*Including* paintbrushes," Tessie said. "Watch now —he's going to eat my paintbrush."

"No, he's not, Tessie," Adam said. "He's just playing. He's very playful."

Adam took a peanut from his pocket and held it out to Q. Q let go of the paintbrush and ate the peanut, shell and all.

"So can we keep him, Tessie?" Adam asked.

Tessie didn't know what to say.

"He's a very little porcupine," Adam said.

"I don't want even little holes in my cabins," Tessie said. "And even if he does prefer peanuts to paintbrushes, he's sure to want to gnaw on wood every now and then."

Adam looked unhappy. Tessie could see how fond he was of the little porcupine.

"What did you say his name was?" Tessie asked.

"Q," Adam said.

"Just Q? What does that stand for?"

"It's like a middle initial," Adam said. "As if his name was Por Q. Pine."

Tessie laughed. "I guess Q stands for Quills then. That's what I'd call him—Mr. Quills."

"If you kept him for your pet, you mean?" Adam said.

Tessie gave up. "Well, all right," she said. "I'll give him a chance. As long as he doesn't eat the cabins. But if he makes one mistake—"

"If he makes a mistake, I'll take him back to the woods," Adam promised.

So Q stayed at the camp with the woodchuck and the owl and the field mouse and the star-nosed mole. Q loved wrestling with the woodchuck, but he was very gentle with the mole and the mouse and the owl.

Tessie inspected her cabins every morning to make sure Q wasn't eating them. And when Q had had the run of the camp for almost two weeks and Tessie had found no holes, she began to feel a little friendlier toward the porcupine—though she still called him *Mr. Quills* in a suspicious tone of voice.

"And don't think I'm going to paint his picture," she told Adam. Tessie was painting the star-nosed mole now, and the porcupine was curled up in a ball watching her.

"I don't feel *that* friendly, Mr. Quills," Tessie explained. "And I don't *absolutely* trust you."

THE DAY Tessie finished her painting of the star-nosed mole, she made some peach ice cream to celebrate. It had fresh peaches and real cream in it, and she made it in a little bucket freezer with a crank on it.

Adam turned the crank, and Tessie packed chunks of ice and rock salt into the bucket. Tessie explained that it was the ice and rock salt together that made the peaches and cream freeze as Adam turned the crank.

The woodchuck and the mole and the mouse and the owl and Q all sat around the freezer watching Tessie and Adam making the ice cream, as if they couldn't wait to have some.

"You can all have some," Tessie said. The owl, she knew, wouldn't eat ice cream, but she put out a dish for him anyway.

When the ice cream was frozen, Adam lifted out the ice-cream can, and Tessie poured the salty ice water over an old stump. Then Tessie dished out seven bowls of ice cream—three very small helpings for the owl and the mouse and the mole.

As Adam passed out the ice cream, Tessie noticed that there was one dish too many. It was because Q was missing.

"Maybe he went to take a nap," Adam said.

But as he spoke there was a loud gnawing sound from the direction of Tessie's cabin. Adam jumped up.

"That's not a field-mouse sound, I guess," he said.

"Certainly not," Tessie said. "And the woodchuck's right here. And the owl and the mole **are**, too. I know

just what that sound is. And so do you." Tessie looked as if she might cry.

"That porcupine's eating my cabin," Tessie said. "That's what he's doing. And just when I was beginning to trust him. I was being as friendly as I could, and here he's sneaked off to eat my cabin. I warned you, Adam."

Adam felt terrible. "Don't feel bad, Tessie," he said. "I'll go get him. I'll take him back to the woods. I'll untame him, and I'll fix the cabin. Please don't feel bad."

And Adam rushed off to find Q before he did too much damage. The gnawing sound was getting louder by the minute.

Adam raced to Tessie's cabin. Right outside the cabin was the porcupine.

Adam shouted for Tessie. Tessie came running, as if she expected to see the cornerposts of the cabin already gnawed in two and the cabin fallen down in a heap.

But Adam was laughing. "Look, Tessie," he called. "Q's not eating the cabin at all. He's just chewing on that old stump!"

It was true. Q was greedily gnawing at an old stump outside Tessie's cabin.

"Well, well," Tessie said. "He's *not* eating the cabin. Well, well. I'd just as soon he'd eat that old stump. I'm always tripping over it."

"He acts as if it tastes a lot better than a cabin," Adam said.

"Hmmm," Tessie said. "Now why didn't I think of that before? That stump *does* taste better than a cabin."

"How do you know?" Adam asked.

"That's the stump where I poured out the salty ice water from the ice-cream freezer," Tessie said. "That stump has a nice woody taste like cabins and

a good salty taste like bacon. It's everything a porcupine likes best all in one dish. For goodness sake!"

Adam went over and broke off a piece of the stump
and chewed it. Tessie was right. It had a good salty
taste.

"So I guess I won't have to untame Q," Adam said.

"Well, I don't know," Tessie said. "You can see
for yourself that a porcupine does have a craving to

gnaw on wood, no matter how well you feed him."

"We could make some more ice cream," Adam said, "and pour the salty ice water over another stump."

"I don't have time to make ice cream every day," Tessie said.

"Well, once in a while," Adam said. "I'll help you. And in between, I can make lima beans. They're easy."

"If a porcupine feels like a good gnaw on a nice hard piece of wood, a lima bean isn't going to satisfy him," Tessie said.

"I know," Adam said. "But the water left over from cooking lima beans is salty. And we could pour that on old stumps when we didn't have any salty ice water."

"Why, yes, I suppose we could," Tessie said.

"And if we run out of lima beans," Adam said, "I could make some plain salty water in a pan. I could put about three tablespoons of salt in plain water and pour that on a stump."

"Yes, I guess you could," Tessie said. "There are a lot of old stumps around here that I'd like to get rid of."

"If I were a porcupine," Adam said, "and I had all the salty wood stumps I could eat, I wouldn't bother with plain wood cabins. Would you?"

"Maybe not," Tessie said.

"And a porcupine that cleaned up all your old wood stumps for you would be good to have around, wouldn't he?" Adam asked.

"Maybe," Tessie said.

Adam lifted Q up off the stump. "That's enough stump for today," he said. "Come have some ice cream."

But when Adam and Tessie got back to the table, all the ice-cream dishes were empty. Even the owl's. The woodchuck was just licking Tessie's dish clean.

Tessie laughed at that. "Why you funny old thing!" she said. And she gave the woodchuck another scoop of ice cream. Then she filled a bowl for Adam and one for Q.

Adam looked happily around at all the animals.
"You can keep them all, you know, Tessie," he said,
"—the woodchuck and the owl and the field mouse

and Q—I tamed them all for you. They'll be good company for you when I go home."

Tessie smiled.

"I'll have to take the mole, though," Adam said. "I brought him on the bus, and I don't think he'd want to stay here without me."

"Of course, not," Tessie said. "You can take his picture, too. I painted it for you."

About the Author and Artist

JEAN MERRILL, the author of over twenty books for children, is a former editor of *Literary Cavalcade* and was an Associate Editor of The Bank Street Readers. She lives half the year in New York City and half in an old farmhouse in Vermont where her working day is enlivened by "the endlessly fascinating company of moles, voles, porcupines, woodchucks, deer, and other wild creatures."

The author of such comic fables of our life and times as *The Pushcart War* and *The Black Sheep,* Jean Merrill has also written many books for younger children, two of the most recent being *Here I Come—Ready or Not!* and *How Many Kids Are Hiding on My Block?* published by Albert Whitman and illustrated by Frances Gruse Scott.

FRANCES GRUSE SCOTT, a designer and graphic artist, studied at Carnegie Tech before going to New York where she worked as a free-lance artist. Mrs. Scott now makes her home in Nyack, N.Y. and has an 8-year-old son who draws "any kind of machine" better than she does, and a 10-year-old daughter who can write and illustrate a book in a tenth the time it takes her mother to illustrate one. Mrs. Scott spent childhood summers in a family "camp" in Pennsylvania, not unlike the one in *Please, Don't Eat My Cabin,* where her mother carried on a spirited war against porcupines.

In addition to her collaborations with Jean Merrill, Mrs. Scott recently illustrated *The Fearless Fossil Hunters* by Tom McGowen, also published by Albert Whitman.